BRAM STOKER'S DRACULA

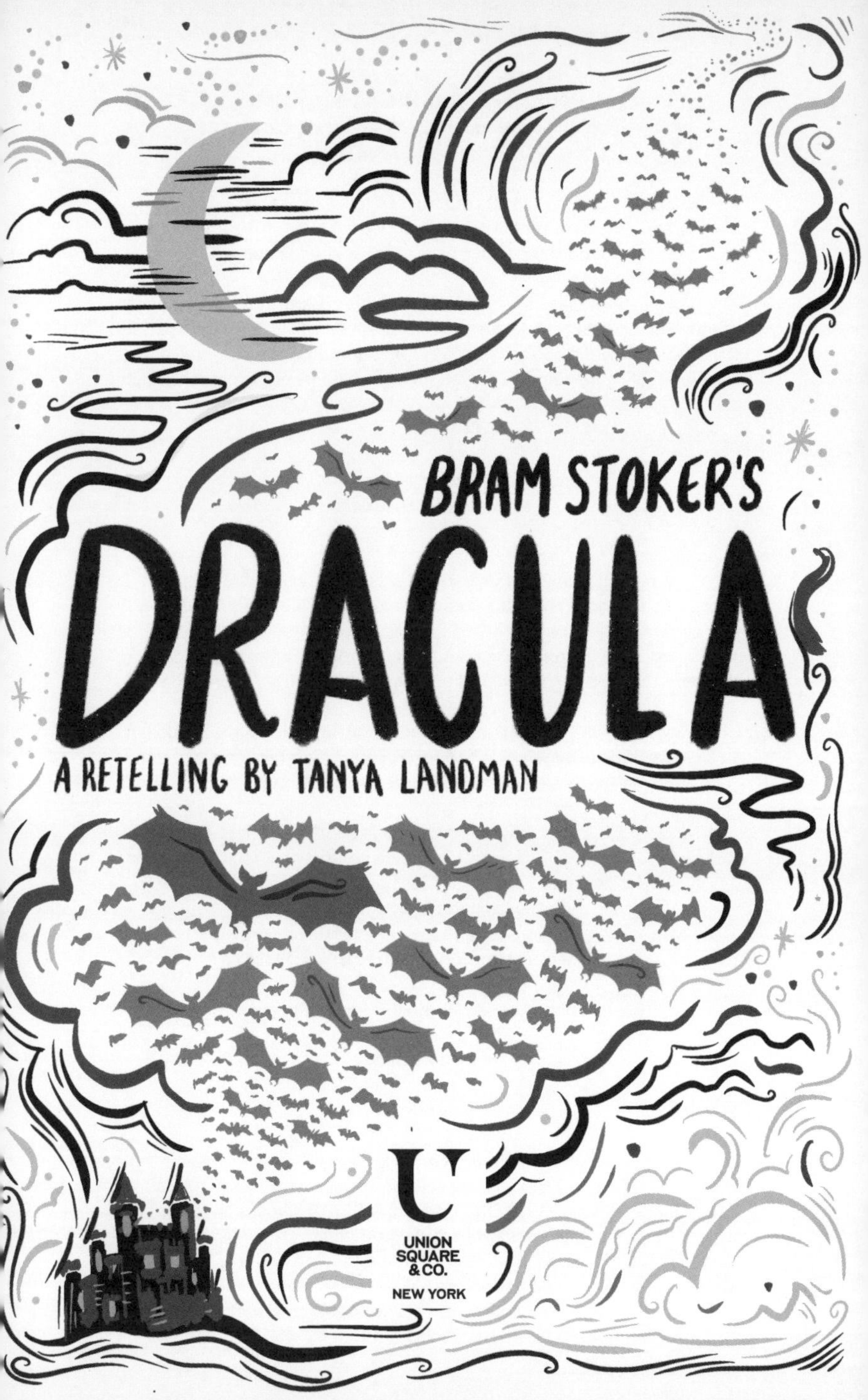
BRAM STOKER'S
DRACULA
A RETELLING BY TANYA LANDMAN
U
UNION
SQUARE
& CO.
NEW YORK

Union Square & Co.
Hachette Book Group
1290 Avenue of the Americas, New York, NY 10104
unionsquareandco.com
@unionsqandco

First published in Great Britain in 2025 by Barrington Stoke Ltd.
First published in the United States and Canada in 2026 by Union Square & Co.

Library of Congress Control Number: 2025938493

ISBN: 978-1-4549-6278-6 (paperback)

Printed in China

03/26
LEO
2 4 6 8 10 9 7 5 3 1

Union Square & Co.'s EVERYONE CAN BE A READER books are expertly written, thoughtfully designed with dyslexia-friendly fonts and paper tones, and carefully formatted to meet readers where they are with engaging stories that encourage reading success across a wide range of age and interest levels.

To Isaac and Jack, for holding my hand through the scary bits

PART 1
DRACULA RISING

Jonathan Harker's Journal

May 3, Bistritz

I have sent a postcard to darling Mina to tell her all is well. I am keeping a full account of my trip to Transylvania in this journal. That way, I can share every detail with her on my return. I wish we were already married! It would be wonderful to see all these new people and places with Mina at my side.

For the last few days, traveling has been pleasant and easy. I have seen charming countryside and lovely towns and cities. But I find myself growing uneasy as I move closer to my destination.

I slept badly last night. My bed was comfortable, but I had all sorts of odd dreams.

Somewhere a dog kept howling as if afraid. Yet today, on I travel, sleep or no sleep. For there is work to be done, and I am the young lawyer my employer has sent to do it! A very rich man named Count Dracula wishes to buy land and property near London. I am to deal with the legal matters and ensure the purchase happens smoothly.

I knew nothing of Transylvania so visited the library before I left England. I read books and looked at maps and discovered that the region is wild and mountainous. Its history is drenched in the blood of centuries of war and conflict. It also seems that every folktale and superstition in the world has its origins in the Transylvanian mountains. I must ask Count Dracula about it all. My stay will be very interesting, I think. I am looking forward to meeting him.

A note was waiting for me at the hotel when I arrived in Bistritz this evening.

Welcome.

Sleep well tonight, my friend. At three tomorrow, the coach will start on the road for Bukovina. A seat on it has been reserved for you. I will send my own carriage to meet you at the Borgo Pass and bring you home to me.

Your friend,
Dracula

May 4, Bistritz

As I checked out of the hotel this morning, the old lady who runs it asked where I was traveling next. I mentioned that I was bound for Count Dracula's castle, and her eyes widened. She took a sharp breath, then she clutched my arm.

"Must you go?" the lady asked. "Do you know what day it is?"

"It is the fourth of May," I said, a little surprised.

"I know that!" she said crossly, and then asked again, "Do you know what day it is?"

"I don't understand . . ." I replied.

"It is the eve of St. George's Day," the lady said. "Tonight, when the clock strikes midnight, all the evil things of the world will be at their most powerful. Do you know where you are going, and what you are going to?"

I told her as gently as I could that I was going on important business and that I could not possibly change my plans. She went down on her knees and begged me not to go. I assured her once more that I could neither abandon nor postpone my journey.

The lady took off the string of beads that held a crucifix from around her neck and insisted on hanging it around mine. I have always believed such things were silly superstition, but the poor lady was so upset that I accepted her gift.

May 5, Castle Dracula

When I left Bistritz yesterday, a small crowd was gathered outside in the street. As I boarded the coach, I heard people muttering to one another. There were all sorts of languages, so I understood very little but picked up the words *Satan*, *Hell*, *werewolf*, and *vampire*. Everyone in the crowd looked at me with pity in their eyes and made the sign of the cross as the coach drove away.

I shared no common language with my fellow passengers, but they all seemed very kind. They insisted on pressing odd gifts into my hands: a bunch of white garlic flowers, a sprig of mountain ash, the blossom of a wild rose. I seem to remember reading that the local tradition is that these things are meant to ward off evil. But surely that is just peasant superstition?

We drove along a winding road past mountains and pine forests. The landscape was spectacular, but there was little time to enjoy it. As the sun sank lower, the coachman drove his horses on and on until we were speeding along so fast it was as if we were in a race with an invisible opponent. My fellow passengers urged the driver to go even faster until at last we stopped at the Borgo Pass, where I was to be collected.

We had arrived early, so there was no one there to meet me. The coachman began insisting he take me on to the next town. But before I could respond, a huge black carriage drawn by four black horses came speeding toward us.

It was driven by a very tall man. He wore a great black hat that hid most of his face. For a moment, I thought I saw a pair of red glowing eyes and sharp white teeth. But I was very tired; I must have been mistaken. The man lifted my luggage from the coach and loaded it onto the carriage. And then he took my arm. He was incredibly strong, and his grip was so tight I dropped all the gifts I had been given. He assisted me up the steps into the carriage and slammed the door. Without another word, we were off, sweeping into the darkness.

It was a very long journey, and I must have fallen asleep. I must have dreamed that the carriage was surrounded by ravenous wolves and that the horses screamed and plunged in terror. I must have dreamed that the driver simply raised his hand as if in command and that the wolves melted away, whimpering. And yet those dreams seemed so real!

I woke from my nightmare when the carriage pulled up in the courtyard of a vast, half-ruined castle. Its tall, black windows cast no rays of light, and its broken battlements were a jagged line against the moonlit sky.

May 5, continued

The driver assisted me down from the carriage, and I felt again the dreadful strength of his grip. Once he had unloaded my luggage, he drove off. I was left alone in the moonlight outside a huge oak door studded with iron nails. There was no knocker, no bell, no sign of any life within. What was I to do?

Panic tightened my chest. What sort of place had I come to? What kind of people lived here? What sort of grim adventure had I set out on?

I had only recently qualified as a lawyer and had very little experience. Was this a normal event in the life of someone in my profession?

I stood motionless, thoughts whirling about my head. Then I heard footsteps from within the castle—a slow, heavy tread, getting closer. When the footsteps stopped, I heard the rattling of chains, then the creak of a bolt being drawn back and a grating rasp as the door was heaved open.

There stood a very tall old man—deathly pale, white-haired, dressed all in black. "Welcome to my home!" he said. "Enter freely and of your own will!"

The instant I stepped over his threshold, he took my hand. He shook it so firmly I almost cried out in pain and shock. His palm was as icy cold as a dead man's.

"Count Dracula?" I asked.

"I am indeed Dracula. I bid you welcome, Mr. Harker."

It was late, Dracula said, and his servants were in bed. He told me he would see to my comfort himself. He carried my bags, showed me my room, then served me with an excellent supper. Dracula ate nothing himself but assured me he had dined earlier.

Once my stomach was full, I felt more relaxed. But later, as we sat talking, I began to notice other odd things that made me uneasy. The Count's hands were unnaturally pale, and there were hairs growing in the center of his palms. His fingernails were very long, trimmed to a sharp point like claws.

As he leaned toward me, I could not help but shudder. His breath smelled so foul that a wave of nausea washed over me. The Count noticed my revulsion and drew back with a grim smile that exposed his sharp, white teeth.

Suddenly, from the valley below, came the howling of many wolves.

"Children of the night," Dracula murmured, his eyes gleaming. "What music they make!"

I did not respond. He said, "You must be tired. The sun will soon be rising, and your bed awaits. Sleep deeply, dream sweetly. I shall be away until the evening. You may rest in peace for as long as you wish."

May 7, early morning

Yesterday, I slept very late indeed. When I finally got up and dressed, I went into the room where I had eaten supper the night before. A cold meal had been laid out for me, and a pot of coffee was keeping warm by the fire. I ate and drank, and once I had finished, I searched for a bell, intending to call a servant to clear the table. But there wasn't one. I went out into the hall looking for a maid or footman but could find no one.

It was not the only thing that struck me as strange as I roamed about the castle that day. The place is furnished with fine, expensive things. Tapestries hang from the walls that must be centuries old. They remind me of ones I have seen in the stately homes of England, but those were all faded and moth-eaten. Dracula's are as brightly colored as they must have been when they were first woven. Yet in all this grandeur there is not a single mirror! I had to find the one I had brought with me before I could brush my hair.

I found many of the doors in the castle were locked, but eventually I discovered a library. It contained a vast number of books about England and a large map. London had been circled in pen and so had Whitby on the coast of Yorkshire for some reason.

I selected a book, sat myself down, and was reading when the Count walked in.

He was very pleasant company, and we talked for a long time about England and his forthcoming move there. He was clearly looking forward to it with great enthusiasm.

"I long to go through the crowded streets of your mighty London," the Count exclaimed. "To be in the midst of the whirl and rush of humanity! To share its life, its change, its death, and all that makes it what it is!"

It felt natural to turn to the business that had summoned me here. The Count had written to my law firm some time ago listing what he required in a property. After a long search, I had found a place called Carfax, which seemed to meet all his needs. I explained to the Count that Carfax House is old and large, and its gardens very extensive. On one side, the land borders the grounds of a mental asylum, but that building is very far distant, and all the patients are kept safely under lock and key. The Count would have the total privacy he desires. Yet the Carfax estate is also within very easy reach of central London—one of his demands. He was delighted with my description of it and signed all the necessary papers.

The Count took them away, saying that he would see they were posted back to my firm in

England as soon as possible. When he returned, he led me to the room where my supper had been laid out on the table. Again, there were no servants present, and again, he said he'd eaten earlier but sat with me as I dined. He asked so many questions about England and English ways and customs that we talked until nearly dawn. The moment he noticed the sky lightening, the Count leaped to his feet and abruptly left the room.

May 8

I have tried telling myself that my rising fear is just the result of exhaustion and lack of sleep. I had many days of travel followed by two full nights of staying up and talking with the Count. It's no wonder that my imagination has begun to run riot!

And yet . . . and yet . . . there is something so strange about this place!

I slept very little last night. When I got up, I hung my little mirror by the window and began to shave. Suddenly, I felt a hand grip my shoulder.

"Good morning!" the Count boomed in my ear.

I was so shocked that I cut myself with my razor. I had not seen him coming. Why not? My face was reflected in my shaving mirror. The whole room behind me was shown in that same reflection. I could feel the Count's hand on my shoulder and feel his rank breath upon my neck. But I could not see him in the mirror.

Impossible! I spun around, and there he was. I glanced back at the mirror. I had to force myself to believe what I could see with my own eyes. Count Dracula had no reflection.

My cut had begun to bleed. The Count saw the trickle of red running down my cheek, and his eyes suddenly gleamed with what looked like a demon's fury. He went to grab my throat, but his hand closed on the string of beads and crucifix that the hotel's landlady had given me a few days ago. At once, his fury passed.

"Take care not to cut yourself again," the Count said quietly. "It is more dangerous than you think in this country. Transylvania is not England."

He took my shaving mirror and hurled it out of the window. I watched it fall and shatter into a thousand pieces on the stones of the courtyard below.

Once more, I ate alone. I have never seen the Count eat or drink, and it is another thing that puzzles me and makes me uneasy. When I had finished my breakfast, there was nothing for me to do but wander around the castle.

I came to a room that looks toward the south. The view was magnificent. From there, I could see that the castle stands on the edge of a precipice. A shaving mirror hurled from that window would fall a thousand feet before it hit the ground! Ahead, a forest spread for as far as I could see, a river winding through it like a silver thread.

I stood admiring the landscape for some time. Then it occurred to me that I could go outside and walk among those trees, breathe the fresh air, and feel the sun on my face.

I set off to find a way out.

There were doors, doors, doors everywhere, but every single door that led outside was locked and bolted.

The castle is a veritable prison, and I am a prisoner!

I was gripped by wild panic. For some time, I behaved much as a rat does in a trap, running here and there, desperate as I looked for a means of escape. When I was certain there was none, I started walking back to my room to puzzle out what was to be done. Yet when I reached it, I did not open the door more than a fraction. I could hear someone moving about inside. I peeped through the crack and saw the Count making my bed as if he were a housemaid. It confirmed what I suspected—there are no servants in Castle Dracula. He himself was the carriage driver who brought me here.

The Count and me. The pair of us. Alone.

What does he mean to do with me?

May 12

For the past few days, Dracula and I have moved carefully around each other like partners in a dance. He knows I am his prisoner but says nothing. I pretend there is nothing wrong. We are polite to each other. Every evening, I engage him in conversation, and he is charming. I ask the Count about the history of Transylvania, and he talks with passion of princes and power, invasions and conquests, victories and defeats—as if he himself had been at every bloody battle.

In return, he asks me about aspects of the English legal system and our laws relating to land and property, imports and exports. The Count wishes to know everything he can about our customs and habits and modes of speech. At times, I have felt as if he is sucking out every last drop of the information in my head!

But tonight was different.

Tonight, there were no questions. Only instructions.

The Count told me to write to my employer telling him I would be staying as a guest at Castle Dracula for another month.

What could I do but obey?

Later

After the Count had gone, I wandered about the castle, still desperate to find a way out, or at least another human being who might help me. I stopped for a moment by an open window. I was looking with longing at the view outside when my attention was caught by something. The Count's head was peering out from a window far below me. He glanced from left to right but did not look up, so he had no idea I was watching him.

I was a little amused to be spying on him to begin with, but then he emerged from the window, headfirst. The Count crawled down the castle wall like a gigantic lizard, his cloak spreading out around him like a pair of great black wings.

May 16

God preserve my sanity! I have no living soul to talk to and must write it down here so that the horror will not drive me mad.

I wandered about the castle again this afternoon and found a room that had the most beautiful view from the window. I settled in a chair and lay back to gaze with longing at the mountains, the trees, the running river. I suppose the calm loveliness of the scenery lulled me to sleep. I hope what happened next was a dream, but I fear it was as real as I am.

Time had passed. I was still in the chair, in the room, at the window, but day had turned to night.

I was not alone.

There were three young women. Two were dark-haired and dark-eyed like the Count. The third woman was fair, with masses of golden hair and eyes like pale sapphires. I seemed somehow to know her face, and to know it in connection with some dreamy fear. But could not remember how or from where.

All of the women were beautiful. All had brilliant white teeth that shone like pearls against the ruby red of their lips. Moonlight streamed through the window behind them, but the women cast no shadow.

I lay motionless, as if asleep, but looked at them from beneath my eyelashes. I felt deadly fear. But I also felt longing. I felt in my heart a wicked, burning desire that they would kiss me with those red lips. It is not good to write this down. Someday Mina might read these words. They would give her such pain! And yet they are the truth.

They whispered together in voices that were diabolically sweet. Then they laughed—a sound so bewitching it was almost painful.

"You go first," one of them said to the fair woman. "We will follow."

"He is young," the fair woman replied. "Strong. There will be kisses for us all."

She approached and bent over me. Her breath was honey-sweet on my neck. She licked her lips like an animal, her red tongue lapping her sharp white teeth. She paused. My skin began to tingle. I felt the soft, shivering touch of those full lips on the tender skin of my throat, and the hard press of two sharp teeth, just touching, lingering there. I closed my eyes and waited . . .

At that moment, the Count stormed into the room. He grabbed the fair woman's neck in his steel-like grip and hurled her from me, his eyes blazing like hellfire.

"How dare you touch him when I had forbidden it?" the Count demanded. "This man belongs to me!"

But a heartbeat later, he seemed to change his mind, as he said, "When I have finished with him, you shall kiss him as much as you wish. But now you must go."

"Are we to have nothing tonight?" one of the women asked.

It was then that I noticed the Count had deposited a sack upon the floor. It moved as if there were some living thing inside. One of the women jumped toward it and from within came the gasp of a half-smothered child.

With glee and hunger, the three women took the sack and faded, disappearing into the moonlight like mist. Horror overcame me, and I sank down, unconscious.

May 19

Last night, Dracula gave me more instructions. He dictated three more letters for me to write to my employer. The first was dated June 12, saying my work for the Count was almost complete and that I would soon return to England. The second, dated June 19, said that I was starting my journey home. The third, dated June 29, declared that I had left the castle and arrived safely in Bistritz.

I fear the twenty-ninth of June will be my last day alive.

God help me!

May 31

I woke up to find my luggage had been taken from my room. The suit in which I traveled, my hat, my overcoat, train schedules, money, maps, and anything that might be useful to me in the outside world—all have been removed.

June 17

This morning, I heard a cracking of whips and the pounding of horses' hooves. I hurried to the window and saw two great wagons driving into the yard. They carried huge wooden boxes that were the size and shape of coffins. They were unloaded by a group of men who all wore the same wide hats, nail-studded belts, sheepskin coats, and high boots. I called down to the men, begging and pleading for help, but all they did was point at me, laugh, and turn away.

June 24

Tonight, I watched the Count emerge from his window again and crawl down the wall. He was not dressed in his great black cape but in my stolen suit.

I can see his plan as clearly as if he had told me. He will allow people to glimpse what appears to be me. There will be "witnesses" to swear that I left his castle, posted my letters, and started on my journey home. But after the twenty-ninth of June, I will disappear from the face of Earth.

Mina—darling Mina—will never know what has happened to me!

It will break her heart.

June 29

This evening, the Count told me with a charming smile, "Tomorrow, my friend, we must part. My carriage shall take you to the Borgo Pass, and there you will board the coach to Bistritz."

“Why can’t I go tonight?” I demanded.

“Because my coachman and horses are away,” he lied smoothly.

“I can walk then,” I said. “I wish to leave. Now. At once.”

The Count said that he was sorry I wished to leave so suddenly but that of course he would never dream of keeping me here against my will! He took a lamp and led me down stairs and along passages to the huge front door. He unbolted and opened it.

And outside—all at once—the howling of wolves filled the night air. They were already close. Coming closer. Getting louder. More frenzied.

Was this the Count’s plan? Was I to be fed to them? Ripped apart?

“Close the door!” I cried, covering my face with my hands to hide my bitter tears of disappointment. The Count threw it shut, and the great bolts clanged and echoed across the hall as they shot back into place.

June 30, dawn

Waking up to daylight gives me hope. Wolves are creatures of the night—so if I leave now, at once, if I walk all day, perhaps I have a chance of escape?

The front door was locked. There must be a key. Where would the Count keep it? In his room? He leaves the castle through his window. Can I get into his room that way?

Later

I made the attempt. It was a terrifying climb across the castle wall to his window. Once inside his room, I could not find the key anywhere. But there was a door in one corner that was not locked. It opened onto stairs that curled downward, which I followed. At the bottom was a dark passage. I felt my way along until at last I came to an old chapel.

Inside the room was a huge box like the ones I had seen unloaded from the wagon. Its lid was askew, so I looked in.

The horror!

The Count lay there asleep, looking so much younger. His white hair and his moustache had turned a dark and glossy black.

Clots of fresh blood spattered his lips. Blood ran over his chin and neck.

He had gorged on some poor soul and now lay there like a filthy leech. Dear God! I was helping the Count on his way to London! For centuries to come, he could satiate his lust for blood among its teeming millions! He would create a new and ever-widening circle of semi-demons to feed upon the helpless inhabitants!

A voice screamed inside my head. *No—it must not happen. I must destroy him!*

I seized the only weapon I could find—a shovel—and lifted it high. But as I struck the Count, his head turned, and he stared at me with a grin of such malice that I fled.

I am going to leave the castle now. I will go the way the Count does and climb down that terrible wall. If I fall into the abyss, I will die, but I will at least die a man. God willing, my soul will rise to heaven.

Goodbye, Mina!

PART 2
THE COUNT FLIES HIS NEST

Mina's Journal

May 24

Jonathan's employer had a letter from him recently saying that he is staying as a guest at Castle Dracula for another month. Yet he has sent nothing directly to me—not a note, not a letter. I have had no word since the card Jonathan posted in Bistritz saying all was well. I suppose he is very busy, but I wish he would write and let me know when he is coming home. I am longing to see him and hear all his news!

When he left for Transylvania, I almost envied him. I thought it must be so nice to see different countries, and I wondered if we would travel together when we are married. I spent hours imagining the two of us seeing new people and places and learning all about them. But hours have turned into days, and days have turned into weeks. There is still nothing from Jonathan, and I am getting more and more anxious.

A letter from my friend Lucy arrived today, which was a welcome distraction.

The dear, sweet girl has had three marriage proposals from three different men in one day! She is giddy with her success, yet she also feels terribly sorry for the two men she had to turn down. "Why can't they let a girl marry three men, or as many as want her, and save all this trouble?" she wrote to me.

Lucy's triumph does not in the least surprise me. Ever since we were children, she has captivated everyone she meets.

The first to ask for her hand was a Dr. Seward. She described him as being "frightfully clever and very important." It seems he runs a mental asylum just outside London for poor souls who are troubled in their minds and is very serious about his work.

Her second suitor was a man named Quincey Morris, an American from Texas. He has told her stories of the wild frontier, of wicked outlaws, valiant cowboy, and gallant heroes that have made her head spin!

The third proposal was from Mr. Arthur Holmwood.

Lucy says Arthur is not frightfully clever like Dr. Seward and does not tell thrilling stories like Quincey Morris. But it is Arthur whom Lucy loves with all her heart and soul, and Arthur whom she has agreed to marry.

How different our lives will be then! Arthur Holmwood will become a lord when his father dies. One day, Lucy will be a lady! They will be terribly grand people moving in the highest tiers of society with an army of servants. As for Jonathan and I . . . our life together will be one of good, steady work. I will have to give up my teaching post when we marry, but I am learning shorthand and typing so that I can assist Jonathan in his office whenever my household duties permit. Despite the difference in our social stations, I am sure that nothing can or will change the friendship between Lucy and I.

I do hope the same is true of Dr. Seward, Mr. Morris, and Mr. Holmwood. I gather from Lucy's letter that the three men have been great friends in the past. I hope for all their sakes that their rivalry over Lucy will not divide them in the future.

July 24, Whitby

I have traveled to Whitby for a little holiday with Lucy and her mother, Mrs. Westenra.

Whitby is a lovely place. Lucy and I have developed a habit of climbing all the steps and sitting on a bench in St. Mary's churchyard. It's at the very top of town, and from there we can see across the rooftops, over the harbor and out to sea.

Lucy is very happy about her engagement and talks of little else. I am so pleased for her, but it has made me somewhat heartsick. I haven't heard from Jonathan for so long. I hope nothing is the matter. I wonder where he is and whether he is thinking of me.

July 26

Yesterday, Jonathan's employer forwarded on a note that Jonathan had written to him from Castle Dracula saying that he was starting for home. It was in Jonathan's handwriting but was just one line. The tone was so odd, so very unlike him, it has made me terribly uneasy.

And now, in addition to my concern for Jonathan, I am beginning to worry about Lucy. She is walking in her sleep again—an old childhood habit. She and I are sharing a room, and I have taken to locking the door at night so Lucy cannot wander away.

July 27

No news from Jonathan, and Lucy's sleepwalking has worsened. I am woken by her every night, and the lack of sleep is making me unwell.

August 3

Another week and still nothing from Jonathan. Where can he be? I do hope he is not ill!

Besides the sleepwalking, there is now an oddness to Lucy that I don't understand. She has become withdrawn. Suspicious. Even in her sleep, she seems to be watching me. I lock the door of our room each night, but in her sleep she tries to open it. When she finds she cannot, she goes around the room searching for the key.

August 6

It's been three more days without news.

Anxiety eats away at me. Lucy is more restless than ever, and a storm is brewing.

Today, I was out walking on the cliffs when I happened to meet a member of the coast guard who was watching a Russian ship being tossed by wind and waves in the bay.

"I can't work it out," he told me in distress. "That ship is being steered mighty strangely, changing about with every puff of wind. Can't her captain see the storm's coming? Why doesn't she come into the harbor?"

August 10

It said in the newspaper that the storm we have endured these past few days is one of the greatest ever recorded. I can well believe it, for it has resulted in something very strange.

The Russian ship I saw from the cliffs continued to be blown back and forth across the bay, and everyone thought it would be dashed to pieces on the rocks. But a sudden change in the wind drove it safely into the harbor. As it came in, people saw it was steered by a dead man who had lashed himself to the ship's wheel.

The moment the ship beached on a bank of sand and gravel, a huge black dog sprang from the deck. It fled through the town, up the steps toward St. Mary's churchyard.

Later, when the ship was examined, they found the cargo hold contained nothing but a number of huge coffin-like wooden boxes.

The ship's logbook revealed a story of horror. During its voyage, the vessel was smothered day after day in unnatural fog. Its crew members disappeared night after night, one by one, until only the captain remained. He tied himself to the wheel with his crucifix and beads, as he would not abandon his ship even in death.

The people here consider the captain to be a hero. He is to be given a public funeral this morning.

Later

From our bench in the churchyard, Lucy and I watched the captain's coffin being carried through the town and up the steps. He was laid to rest in a grave near us, and poor Lucy was terribly upset.

Indeed, she was so very distressed I can't help thinking that her sleepwalking is affecting her mind. I shall take her for a long walk this afternoon. Perhaps if I tire her out, Lucy will sleep soundly tonight.

Later, 11 p.m.

It has worked. Lucy is asleep and breathing softly.

August 11

I have passed a terrible, terrible night! I woke suddenly, overwhelmed by fear. Moonlight streamed into our room, and when I looked across it, I saw Lucy's bed was empty! The door was shut but not locked. Somehow, she had found the key and let herself out.

I went to find her, hoping she was in the house, but the front door was wide open. The church clock was striking one as I ran along the streets toward the steps leading up to the churchyard. Lucy and I have so often walked that way I thought her feet may have carried her there all by themselves. I was still some distance away when I saw a white figure on our bench.

Lucy! I thought. *In her nightgown! But who is that?*

A dark figure was bent over her. When I called Lucy's name, it raised its head. I had a brief glimpse of a white face and gleaming red eyes.

When I reached Lucy, she was alone, asleep, but her breath came in long, heavy gasps. I had to shake Lucy very hard to wake her. I threw my shawl around her and fastened it at her throat with a safety pin. But I must have been very clumsy, for this morning I see that I pricked through a fold of her skin and there are two tiny wounds in her neck.

August 13

I woke in the night to see Lucy sitting up in bed, pointing to the window. Outside, a great bat was whirling in circles. Seeing me, it flew away across the harbor. Lucy lay down again and slept peacefully for the rest of the night.

August 14

I passed a pleasant day with Lucy and her mother. Toward evening, I went out for a stroll on my own to think and worry about Jonathan. I returned in moonlight and saw Lucy sitting at our open window, her head leaning against the frame. I thought she was looking for me and so I waved, but as I got closer, I realized she was sleeping. On the windowsill beside her was what I took to be a large black bird.

When I reached our room, I closed the window and put Lucy to bed. The dear, sweet creature! She looks very pale and haggard.

August 17

A dreadful gloom is hanging over us. Mrs. Westenra has told me that she has a weak heart and will not live much longer. She does not want Lucy to know, and so I have to keep it secret, which is a heavy burden indeed. Besides that, there is still no news from Jonathan, and Lucy is growing weaker. The tiny wounds at her throat have not healed. In fact, they are larger than before and the edges ragged. Mrs. Westenra says they are nothing to worry about, but unless they heal within a day or two, I shall insist Lucy sees a doctor.

August 19

Joy, joy, joy!

At last, I received news of Jonathan! He has been very ill with a brain fever, but he is alive and in a hospital in Budapest! I am going to him at once.

August 24, Budapest

Jonathan is pale and weak and very disturbed in his mind. It is as if he has suffered a great and terrible shock, but he says he doesn't remember what happened. The nurse tells me he was raving when he was admitted to the hospital but wouldn't tell me what he said. All the nurse did was make the sign of the cross and then put a finger to her lips.

Jonathan has given me his journal for safekeeping. He does not wish to look at it ever again and says its contents are delusions created from his fevered brain. He told me I can read it if I wish, but I have chosen not to. Jonathan does not want to think of the past few months, so neither will I. We will put them behind us and move on.

We were married this afternoon. Jonathan sat in bed, propped up with pillows. He looked so frail, but he said "I will" so firmly and strongly!

It brought tears to my eyes, and I could barely speak my own vows—my heart was so full.

Afterward, I took his journal, wrapped it in a sheet of white paper, and tied it with the blue ribbon from around my neck. I dropped melted wax on the knot and sealed it with the impression of my wedding ring, a visible token of our trust in each other and in our future.

September 22, Exeter, Devon

Jonathan has not kept a journal since we married and returned home, so neither have I. I wished for us to have no secrets from each other. It would have felt like an act of betrayal to write down any worries privately. But now, today, I must put my troubled thoughts into words. As I cannot speak them aloud, I will record them here before I go mad!

Jonathan is not the energetic, fearless, wonderful man he was before he went to Transylvania. Now he is startled by the slightest noise. If a dog howls in the night, Jonathan trembles like a leaf. His dreams are terrible. There have been many times when I've had to shake him awake, but he will never tell me what haunts him.

And today such a strange thing happened!

Jonathan and I were in London. We were walking along the street when he suddenly clutched my arm so tight he has left bruises on my flesh. He went very pale, and his eyes bulged with terror as he gazed across the street. He was looking at a very tall, very thin young man who was staring at a pretty girl sitting in a carriage. I had a good look at him myself. His face was hard and cruel, his teeth pointed like an animal's, his lips blood red.

"Who is that?" I asked Jonathan.

"The man himself!" he said in a whisper.

Just then, the pretty girl's carriage moved off, and the thin young man followed after it. Jonathan started muttering, "It is him! It is the Count! How has he grown young? Oh my God! My God! My God!"

I feared to upset Jonathan more by asking what he meant. Instead, I drew him away toward a park where we sat on a bench beneath a tree. He fell asleep with his head on my shoulder, and when he woke, he had quite forgotten the incident.

It is not the first time Jonathan has lapsed into forgetfulness. I am beginning to wonder if he suffered some sort of brain injury in Transylvania. A terrible thought nags at me. Should I read his journal? Might the contents provide a clue as to how I can help him?

Later

A telegram has come.

Lucy is dead! Gone, gone, never to return to us! She was buried today!

Today.

In London.

While I was there with Jonathan. And I did not know!

How could I not know that Lucy was being laid in her tomb? Lucy—so young, so lovely, so full of life, so beloved. What accident or sickness can have carried her off so quickly? How? How? How can she be dead?

Misery, misery, misery!

PART 3
LUCY'S DEATH

Mina's Journal

September 30, morning

I now know how Lucy died.

I also know that Lucy's death and Jonathan's "brain fever" had the same cause.

What a devastating whirlwind these past few days have been!

What a shocking amount of new information there is for me to try to understand!

I have experienced every emotion possible.

I will write a full account of it here in the order in which it happened. I must be calm. Logical. Sensible. If I can understand and accept past events, then perhaps I will better face what lies in the future.

I begin with Lucy and what happened to her after I left Whitby for Jonathan and Budapest.

When their holiday was over, Lucy and her mother returned home to Hampstead, London. It was not a happy homecoming. Lucy was haunted by strange fears and slept badly every night. She kept being woken by scratching, flapping noises at her window, and her throat hurt constantly.

Her fiancé, Mr. Holmwood, was very worried about her. But he was needed by his dying father's bedside and could not be with Lucy. So he wrote to his old friend Dr. Seward, begging him to examine Lucy and find the cause of her disease.

Dr. Seward visited her but was deeply puzzled by Lucy's illness. He could find no reason for it but had no doubt that she was very unwell. Desperate, he wrote to his old professor in Amsterdam—Dr. Van Helsing.

Dr. Van Helsing is an expert in little-known diseases. He is a man of science but utterly open-minded. He has an interest in ancient folk remedies and charms that most scientists dismiss as mere peasant superstition. Dr. Van Helsing also practices unusual treatments like hypnosis if he feels the occasion calls for it.

Dr. Van Helsing came to see Lucy, but even he could not fathom what was making her ill. He traveled back to Amsterdam, promising to return if her condition worsened.

It did, and very suddenly.

Dr. Van Helsing was summoned back by Dr. Seward at the beginning of September.

When he arrived, the bones of Lucy's face were standing out, and her breathing was painful to hear. She was as pale as chalk, as if she had lost a vast quantity of blood. And yet Lucy had suffered no wound or injury, and it was not the time of her monthly bleed.

Whatever the cause, there was no time to be lost, Dr. Van Helsing said. She must be given a transfusion of blood immediately. But who was to be the donor?

At this point, Mr. Holmwood burst in. Fearing for Lucy's life, he had left his dying father's side and dashed to hers. And so half of Mr. Holmwood's life blood was transferred into Lucy's veins. Afterward, he was told to eat heartily and rest well, and he obeyed the doctors' commands.

Dr. Van Helsing was adjusting Lucy's pillows when the black band of velvet Lucy always wore about her throat slipped. He saw the little wounds

I thought I had made with the safety pin. I had so blamed myself for causing that injury! But those wounds were not my doing.

Dr. Van Helsing said nothing to Dr. Seward about the suspicion those wounds had sparked in his mind. He'd been Dr. Seward's teacher and knew how resistant the younger man was to anything he believed to be "superstitious nonsense."

Dr. Van Helsing returned to Amsterdam that night to consult the books in his library. But before he left, he ordered Dr. Seward to watch over Lucy all night. Dr. Seward must not sleep, he said. And Lucy must not be left alone during all the hours of darkness.

That night, Lucy was extremely tired but fought against sleep. When Dr. Seward asked her why, she said she feared to dream. He promised he'd wake her if he saw any signs of her having nightmares. With a sigh of relief, she sank back on her pillow and slept peacefully until morning.

Dr. Seward had been awake all night but went to work in his mental asylum the following day. One of his patients—an inmate called Renfield—was behaving very strangely. Dr. Seward was becoming increasingly concerned about him. But in the evening, he returned to watch over Lucy as he had promised.

Dear Lucy saw the poor man was exhausted and told him to sleep in the room next to hers. They left both their doors open, and she promised Dr. Seward that she would call out if she became afraid. Dr. Seward slept until Dr. Van Helsing returned from Amsterdam and shook him awake.

Together they went in to see Lucy.

She lay in a dead faint, ghastly pale, her gums shrunk back from her teeth like a corpse. Her heartbeat was very faint.

They lost no time. Another transfusion was carried out, with Dr. Seward now giving half his blood to keep Lucy alive.

That night, Dr. Van Helsing watched over her during the long hours of darkness.

The following morning, a garland of fresh flowers was delivered, which Dr. Van Helsing had ordered for Lucy from abroad. Thinking they were a gift, she was delighted, until she realized they were nothing but wild garlic. Lucy disliked the smell, but he insisted that she wear the garland about her neck that night. He also rubbed garlic leaves around every inch of her window and doorframes. In the evening, Dr. Van Helsing left the house feeling confident that Lucy would sleep safely and wake well with the protections he had put in place.

The two doctors returned at eight o'clock the next morning. Lucy's mother greeted them and said that Lucy was still sleeping soundly.

Dr. Van Helsing was delighted. "My treatment is working!"

But Mrs. Westenra said that Lucy's peaceful night of sleep was due to her. "I was worried about the poor dear in the night, so went in to check on her. She was sleeping, but her room was awfully stuffy, and that horrid stink of garlic was everywhere! I took the flowers away and opened the window so Lucy might breathe some fresh air."

The men said nothing. But when Mrs. Westenra returned to her own room, Dr. Van Helsing broke down. It was a few moments before he summoned the courage to go in and see Lucy.

Lucy was weaker and paler than ever. She needed a third transfusion. This time Dr. Van Helsing's blood was poured into Lucy's veins.

After he had rested and eaten, Dr. Van Helsing gently told Mrs. Westenra that she must not remove anything from Lucy's room without his permission. He assured her that the garlic flowers were medicine and that inhaling their scent was part of Lucy's cure. He said that he himself would watch over Lucy that night and the next, and send for Dr. Seward only when he was required.

On September 17, Dr. Van Helsing had to be in Amsterdam. He sent an urgent telegram to Dr. Seward:

> *WATCH OVER HER TONIGHT. FLOWERS MUST BE WORN. VERY IMPORTANT. DO NOT FAIL.*

The telegram was delivered to Dr. Seward twenty-two hours too late.

Lucy wrote a note that night:

> *I have barely strength but must leave this for Arthur so he knows what happened to me . . .*
>
> *A noise at the window woke me. I called out, but Dr. Seward was not in the next room as Dr. Van Helsing had promised he would be. A huge bat flapped against the glass.*

Maybe its noise woke Mother, for she came in and held me as she did when I was small. The flapping and the banging frightened Mother; I could feel her heart beating terribly hard. Then there was a loud crash of breaking glass, and Mother cried out and clutched at me so wildly she tore off the garland of flowers from around my neck. Mother fell, hitting her head against mine, pinning me upon on my bed.

Her heart stopped beating!

The maids had heard the crash and came running. They lifted poor Mother off me, laid her on my bed and covered her dead body with a sheet. They were so distressed and frightened, I told them to go to the dining room and steady themselves with a glass of wine.

I laid the garland of flowers on Mother's breast, for that is what you are meant to do when someone dies. I recalled what Dr. Van Helsing had said about me wearing them, but I didn't like to take them away from Mother. I thought the maids would sit up with me while the dark hours remained, but they didn't come back. When I went looking, I found them lying on the floor of the dining room, unconscious. What was left of the wine smelled strange, as if it had been drugged. I have come back to sit with Mother alone.

God shield me from harm! I shall hide this note in my pocket. If I die this night, they will find it on my body. Goodbye, Arthur. God keep you, my dearest love, and God help me!

The following morning—September 18—Dr. Seward and Dr. Van Helsing arrived at the Westenras' house at the same time. They had to break in, for the maids had been so heavily drugged they had still not woken.

They found Mrs. Westenra covered in a sheet. It had been blown back in the breeze from the broken window, revealing her dead face frozen with terror. Beside her lay Lucy, her throat bare, her wounds white and mangled, her skin as cold as death.

Yet Lucy still lived.

They acted quickly, reviving the maids, who then lit fires and heated water. Lucy was placed in a warm bath, her hands and feet rubbed.

It was a fight with death, Dr. Seward declared, but Dr. Van Helsing replied, "If it were only a fight with death, I would let her slip away."

After some time, the heat began to take effect. Lucy was lifted from the bath and laid in bed, and one of the maids was set to watch over her. Meanwhile, the men went downstairs to decide what could be done next. Another transfusion was needed. But who could they ask to donate their blood?

They were startled to hear a voice demand, "How about me?"

Quincey Morris, the Texan who'd proposed to Lucy, had arrived amid all the chaos! Arthur Holmwood had telegrammed him about Lucy's illness, and the dear fellow had rushed to her side. He had arrived, they hoped, just in time to save her.

"A brave man's blood is the best thing on this Earth when a woman is in trouble," declared Dr. Van Helsing. And so the operation was carried out once more, but it took longer and had less effect than on previous occasions.

On the night of September 18, the men took turns watching over Lucy while she slept. She did not improve. Her pale gums were drawn back from her teeth, making them look larger than usual, and the canines were longer and sharper than the rest.

When she woke, she asked for Arthur, and they sent for him.

He arrived, and Lucy recovered a little, but she was not expected to live much longer.

On September 20, the wounds on Lucy's throat disappeared.

For a brief moment, Dr. Seward thought that meant she was getting better, but Dr. Van Helsing shook his head.

"She is dying," he explained. "Wake Arthur. He wishes to be with her at the end."

When he came in, Lucy said softly, "Arthur! Oh, my love!"

Arthur went to kiss her, but Dr. Van Helsing stopped him. "Hold her hand," he said. "It will comfort her more."

So Arthur kneeled beside the bed and took Lucy's hand, and gradually she sank back into sleep. Then her breathing became harsh, and in a sort of sleepy daze, she opened her eyes again. They were dull and hard. In a deep voice that none of the men had ever heard before, Lucy demanded, "Kiss me, Arthur!"

He bent toward her, but Dr. Van Helsing dragged him back.

"Not for your life!" he said. "Not for your living soul or hers!"

A jolt of rage and frustration flitted over Lucy's face. Her sharp teeth snapped like a dog's. Then her eyes closed, and she took a couple of heavy breaths. When she opened them again, her eyes were soft and blue and full of love.

She took Dr. Van Helsing's hand in hers and thanked him. "You are my true friend," Lucy told him. Her last words were, "Protect Arthur. Give me peace!"

"I swear it," Dr. Van Helsing said. And then he said Arthur could kiss Lucy but just once and on the forehead. Lucy's eyes closed. Her breathing stopped.

It was over.

Arthur left the room to weep in private, but Dr. Van Helsing continued to watch Lucy's corpse.

Dr. Van Helsing sat. He observed. And he saw that Lucy was not beginning to develop the withered, waxy look of a body starting to decay. After all, a doctor is familiar with death and the changes it makes to a human body.

As Dr. Van Helsing watched, Lucy's youth and beauty began to creep back. Only a few minutes after she had taken her last breath, her face looked softer, her cheeks were lightly flushed and her lips were plump and pink.

"Lucy is at peace at last," Dr. Seward said. "It is the end!"

"Not so, alas!" replied Dr. Van Helsing. "This is only the beginning."

Mr. Holmwood's father died shortly after Lucy, and Arthur became the new Lord Godalming. But the poor man was consumed with grief. When Dr. Van Helsing asked to look through Lucy's papers, Arthur asked no questions but simply nodded.

Dr. Van Helsing read all the letters I had sent her, including one written from the hospital in Budapest in which I described Jonathan's illness. There was another letter that mentioned Lucy sleepwalking in Whitby.

My most recent letter to her was still unopened. When she did not reply to it, I had assumed she was too busy with wedding preparations to write to me! But the poor darling was so ill by then she could not even read it. I had posted it to her when

Jonathan and I arrived back in England. It gave her our address in Exeter.

That is how Dr. Van Helsing knew where to send the telegram telling me of her death.

A day or so later, he wrote to me asking if he might visit. He wished to discuss what had happened to Lucy while I was with her in Whitby.

Dr. Van Helsing called on me on September 25, while Jonathan was away on business.

His visit changed everything.

I was in a state of great unease that day. With Jonathan away from home, I had taken the opportunity of reading his journal and then wished I had left the wretched thing untouched. I was certain the contents could not possibly be true! The things Jonathan described could not have happened. Count Dracula could not be such a foul, unnatural creature! And yet what kind of awful brain fever could create such horror from nothing? How could he imagine those women? How could he long to kiss them? Jonathan was surely suffering a terrible disease of the mind. Could such an illness be treated? Was there a cure?

My mind was buzzing with unasked questions when Dr. Van Helsing arrived.

As he wanted to know about Lucy's strange behavior in Whitby, I had typed a copy of my journal and simply handed it to him.

He was very impressed with my efficiency and so very kind about Lucy. Indeed, his manner toward me was so gentle that later I could not help confessing to him my fears for Jonathan's sanity.

We talked for a long time. Before he left, I typed a copy of Jonathan's journal, which he took away with him to read. The moment he had finished, he sent me a note that turned my world upside down.

Dr. Van Helsing assured me that Jonathan's journal did not contain the delusional ravings of a sick man. He was certain that every word was the truth!

I cannot describe the sense of relief that washed over me. I was so weak with it that I had to sit down. It seemed utterly bizarre to be delighting in the fact that a creature like Count Dracula really existed, yet it was such a great weight off my mind.

As soon as Jonathan came home, I told him about Dr. Van Helsing's visit and showed him the note he had sent.

The impact on Jonathan was far greater than it had been on me! He was like a man reborn—no longer the pale, fragile, nervous wreck that I had married but the energetic, fearless, wonderful man I'd fallen in love with! Because he knew that all he experienced was real and true, that he was not delusional, that his eyes and ears did not mislead him. . . . He could be sure that he could trust his own judgement, and the joy it brought him was beyond words.

The following morning, Jonathan and Dr. Van Helsing met, and we all talked at great length. Dr. Van Helsing was not yet sure what could or should be done about the Count but has told us that a great task lies ahead. We have promised to help him in whatever way we can.

PART 4
AFTERLIFE

Mina's Journal

September 30, continued

It has been my task these past few days to put together a record of all that we know relating to Count Dracula. Our journals, diaries, letters, telegrams, newspaper articles—I have assembled everything in order of date and typed copies so that those of us involved in this dreadful business share the same knowledge. But the account that follows of what happened to Lucy after her death is for myself alone. I feel the need to put my troubled thoughts and feelings into words and write them down so I may better cope with them.

On September 26, after Dr. Van Helsing had left Jonathan and I and was returning to London, a newspaper headline caught his attention.

"A HAMPSTEAD MYSTERY!" it screamed.

The article was about several reports of children disappearing at night and not being found until the following morning. All of the children told the same tale of being led away by what they called "a bloofer lady." ("Bloofer," I suppose, is how they pronounce the word *beautiful* in their local accent.)

The article finished with a line that chilled Dr. Van Helsing's blood. It said that all the missing children returned home with tiny puncture wounds in their throats—the kind that might be made by a rat or a very small dog.

The moment he arrived in London, Dr. Van Helsing went to Dr. Seward and thrust the newspaper in his face.

"What do you make of this?"

Dr. Seward is a scientist of the natural world, not the unnatural. He likes things that can be weighed and measured. Things that can be logically explained. He believed that whatever had injured Lucy had now injured the children.

I imagine the conversation that followed was frustrating for both of them. Dr. Van Helsing had been Dr. Seward's professor. He wanted Dr. Seward to think, to understand, to come to the proper conclusion by himself. But Dr. Seward did not want to face the truth because it was too strange, too ugly. And so the two men talked in circles until Dr. Van Helsing came close to losing his temper.

"You still believe that whatever hurt the children also hurt Miss Lucy?" he demanded.

"There can be no other explanation," Dr. Seward replied.

"You are wrong!" Dr. Van Helsing told him. "It is worse. Far worse. The holes in the children's throats were made *by* Miss Lucy."

Dr. Seward told Dr. Van Helsing that he was mad. Lucy was dead! It was impossible!

"I wish I were mad," Dr. Van Helsing replied. "It would be easier to bear."

Dr. Van Helsing offered to show Dr. Seward proof that Lucy was harming children. And so, under cover of darkness, the two men broke into the Westenra family tomb in Hampstead cemetery.

They found poor Lucy's coffin, and Dr. Van Helsing began to unscrew the lid. Dr. Seward waited for the foul smell of decay, for she'd been dead a week. But there was no smell.

The coffin was empty.

Dr. Seward blamed body-snatchers. They had taken her away, he said. Sold Lucy's corpse to some doctor or other for dissection! Dr. Seward still could not—would not—face the awful truth. But Dr. Van Helsing persuaded him to watch and wait for what remained of the night.

They took up their hiding places. It was past two in the morning when they spotted a white figure flitting across the graveyard and entering the Westenra tomb. They followed, and once more, Dr. Van Helsing unscrewed the lid of Lucy's coffin.

And there she lay, even more beautiful than she had been while she lived. Dr. Van Helsing pulled back Lucy's blood-red lips and showed Dr. Seward her pointed canine teeth.

"Do you believe me now, my friend?" Dr. Van Helsing asked.

Dr. Seward declared that someone had put her body back when they were not looking!

Dr. Van Helsing said very gently, "Most people do not look so healthy seven days after their death."

It was a fact that Dr. Seward could not deny. He had to accept that Lucy, the dear, sweet girl he loved and had once wished to marry, had become a vampire. She was one of the Undead.

A dreadful task now lay ahead, Dr. Van Helsing told Dr. Seward. They could not save her mortal life, but they could perhaps still save her immortal soul. To do that, her Undead body must be killed while she lay asleep in her coffin. Her head must be cut off. Her mouth must be filled with garlic.

And there was more.

The man Lucy had chosen to marry, the man to whom Lucy had given her heart, would have to drive a stake through that same organ.

Poor Arthur!

If Dr. Seward had struggled to believe the truth, how unbearable would it be for him?

Last night, the night of September 29, Lord Arthur Godalming, Quincey Morris, Dr. Seward, and Dr. Van Helsing visited the graveyard. They watched. Waited. And at last a white figure came toward the tomb.

It was Lucy, but oh, how changed!

They advanced on her, and Dr. Van Helsing held up his lantern. Her lips were crimson with fresh blood that trickled from her mouth to chin.

Lucy snarled and stared at them, her eyes full of fire. Then she crooned sweetly, "Come to me, Arthur. My arms hunger for you. Come, my love."

Arthur must have been under the same vampire's spell as Jonathan when he'd felt such wicked longing for the three women in Castle Dracula. Arthur moved forward, arms open, but Dr. Van Helsing stepped between him and Lucy. He thrust a crucifix toward her face, making her recoil and flee to her tomb.

After that, the men did all that was necessary. As Lucy lay sleeping in her coffin, Arthur took a stake and pressed the point into her white flesh. He hammered it home with all his might.

She gave a blood-curdling screech, but Arthur drove the stake deeper and deeper. He never faltered. Face set, he did his duty.

It was a terrible task.

But once it was done, a calm came over her wasted face and form. Arthur bent and kissed her, and then he and Quincey Morris left the tomb. It was left to the two doctors to remove Lucy's head and fill her mouth with garlic.

I hope the men took no pleasure in their task, and it was done in pity, not in triumph. I must confess that I was disturbed by the account in Dr. Seward's diary of the events of last night when I typed them up for our records this morning. He described all his love for Lucy turning to "icy hate" when he saw her "sweet purity transformed to foul lust." He described her as a "Thing"—"a devilish mockery" of what she had once been. There seemed to be a savage relish in her destruction.

But my feelings are unimportant. All that matters is that Lucy's eternal soul has been freed from its prison. She is at peace now.

For Dr. Van Helsing, Dr. Seward, Lord Godalming, Quincey Morris, Jonathan, and myself? Lucy's end is our beginning.

Ahead lies a task that binds the six of us as tightly as any warriors that have ever gone into battle.

Count Dracula still walks the earth.

The six of us have sworn to hunt him down and put an end to him.

PART 5
MINA'S FATE

Mina's Journal

September 30, late evening

Dr. Seward has an apartment in the mental asylum he runs, which has become our headquarters. We have formed ourselves into a sort of committee with Dr. Van Helsing as our head. Tonight, I sat at his side to act as secretary.

"This is not a mere matter of life or death, my friends," Dr. Van Helsing told us at the start of our meeting. "If we lose, we will become like Dracula. He will make us the Undead: foul things of the night without heart or conscience, who will prey on the bodies and souls of those we once loved best. They in turn will prey on others, and it will go on and on until the whole of humanity is the same. We must not fail."

We needed no reminding that the enemy we face is unlike any other. I knew from Jonathan's journal that the Count is stronger than any mortal man. Tonight, I learned that Dracula had been a great warrior when he'd been alive—I mean truly alive, as a human being. He'd led his armies into battle with an iron will and a determination to conquer. That ruthlessness still burns in him, and he is now more cunning than ever. He has developed that skill over centuries.

Besides all that, Dracula can change his shape to a bat or a great black dog, as he did when he jumped from the deck of the ship in Whitby. He can summon storms and conjure fog, as he did on the dreadful voyage that killed that poor sea captain. He can command wolves and all the creatures of the darkness. And he can disappear into a shaft of moonlight just as those dreadful vampire women did in Castle Dracula.

How can we fight such an enemy? It seems impossible!

Yet Dr. Van Helsing believes it can be done.

There are two ways, he says, that we might win:

1) It seems that if the Count is awake at sunrise, he becomes trapped in the form of a man until the sun sets. During those hours of daylight, he is much, much weaker and can be fought and killed like any mortal man—so if we find him then, we can surely defeat him. It is why the Count prefers to sleep in his coffin-bed during the day.

2) Our second option is to find that coffin-bed in which he sleeps and do to him what was done to Lucy.

This second option is fraught with difficulty, for *which* coffin-bed does he sleep in? There are so many possibilities!

Things that made no sense to me before have begun falling into place like the pieces of a puzzle. All those coffin-shaped boxes that Jonathan saw being unloaded at Castle Dracula! There were fifty of them in total. Those same fifty boxes were brought to England as cargo on the dead sea captain's ship. Jonathan has discovered that they were all carried from Whitby over land to Carfax, the estate he helped the Count purchase.

From Carfax, they may have gone on to other destinations that we do not yet know of.

It is lucky for us that the Carfax estate borders the grounds of Dr. Seward's mental asylum. Our work begins here, from our base in his rooms.

The plan is to break into Carfax, see how many coffin-boxes remain there, and discover the exact locations of the rest. When they are all found, Dr. Van Helsing will purify every one of them by placing sacred Holy Communion wafers inside. Once they are purified in this way, Dracula will not be able to hide or sleep in them.

We were discussing the details of who should do exactly what when Quincey Morris got up quietly and left the room. A few moments later, there was the crack of a pistol shot, and the window shattered.

It seemed Mr. Morris had noticed a huge bat crouching on the windowsill. He had crept out, meaning to kill it, but his bullet missed, and the creature flew away. Mr. Morris had just come back in when Dr. Van Helsing said to me, "You are too precious, Madam Mina, to risk coming with us. You must stay here. We will work better if we know you are in no danger."

All the men—even Jonathan—nodded in agreement.

It was a bitter pill for me to swallow. I wanted to protest, yet I dared not for fear they would leave me out of future discussions altogether.

The men have gone off to Carfax house to do their work, leaving me behind for my own safety.

Jonathan Harker's Journal

October 1, 5 a.m.

I have never seen Mina looking so strong and well. I am glad she let us go without complaint. It has worried me to have her involved in all this, but her part is finished. She has typed and organized the record of events thus far and must now step back.

Before we entered the Carfax house, Van Helsing gave each of us protections against Dracula: a crucifix to wear about our necks, a wreath of garlic flowers, and an envelope containing a piece of Holy Communion wafer. Seward had brought with him a set of skeleton keys and soon had the door opened. We each carried a lamp. As we entered, odd shadows flicked about. I could not escape the feeling that someone else was there among us.

Slowly, we edged along corridors, making our way through the house to its chapel.

In truth, we did not need the lamps. Our noses would have led us there if we had been in the pitch-dark.

None of the others had met the Count face to face. They were not prepared for his smell. It had been bad enough when I had seen him in his castle. Here in Carfax—how can I describe the stench? It was like every foul thing combined and made worse—as if rot itself had rotted. It sickened all of us, yet we persisted. At last, we found the boxes, but there were only twenty-nine of them.

We began to look for the others, or at least for information as to where they may have been sent. I suddenly thought I saw the Count's white face, his red eyes, his red lips, but when I held up my lamp, there was nothing.

Then came a great rushing sound, and the place swarmed with rats. Lord Godalming had thought to bring his dogs with him. He whistled, and the terriers came running, barking loudly, and got to work. When they had finished, it felt as if an evil presence had departed.

"Our night has been successful," Van Helsing told us when we left Carfax. "And it has been done without bringing dear Madam Mina into it. I am glad she has not been troubled by horrors she might never forget."

We returned to Seward's living quarters. I entered our room on tiptoe and found Mina so deeply asleep she did not stir. She looked paler than usual.

The other men were right. I had been sure that Mina should take a full part in this, but they persuaded me otherwise, and I am grateful to them. Seeing her so exhausted, I realize this task is too great a strain for a woman.

Later

I slept until the sun was high in the sky and woke refreshed. But Mina was still exhausted. When I shook her gently awake, she did not recognize me for a moment or two—she just stared with a blank look on her face. She then complained of being very tired, so I let her rest. We men have work to do. The remaining boxes must be traced.

Mina's Journal

October 1

Jonathan has not said a word about what happened in Carfax last night. He has confided in me for so many years that to see him silent on such an important matter is very painful. I know this secrecy comes from his great love and his desire to protect me, yet I am crying about it like a fool!

Last night, I went to bed because I had been told to. I felt like a small child being sent away by the grown-ups. For a long time, I couldn't sleep. I remember hearing the barking of dogs, and then there was a silence over everything.

I got up and looked out of the window. A thin streak of white mist was wafting across the grass toward the house and then rising up the walls. When I went back to bed, a great weariness washed over me. I fell asleep and dreamed that the mist had poured into the room and grown thicker and thicker until it formed a sort of column with a livid white face and two red eyes. It bent over me, and I was so terrified I fainted.

I never want to dream like that again! Tonight, I will try hard to sleep naturally. But if I do not,

I must ask Dr. Seward to prescribe me a sedative that will give me an easy, dreamless sleep.

October 2, 10 p.m.

I have taken the sedative and am waiting for sleep. I hope I haven't done the wrong thing. I am beginning to wonder if I was foolish to take away the power of waking.

Jonathan Harker's Journal

October 2, evening

It has been a long and difficult day. However, using various tricks and strategies and a little bribery, I have made several discoveries. Shortly after the Count arrived in England, he purchased a London townhouse, and this, I believe, may contain all the remaining boxes.

I have the address, but how are we to gain access? Carfax was easy to break into—it is so secluded, there was no one to see us enter or leave the place. But in the middle of London? We would be taken for thieves!

I wish I could talk it over with Mina but must not involve her!

She is sleeping very soundly, but her forehead has creased into little wrinkles as if she is thinking even in her sleep.

She is still very pale.

October 3, early morning

We have passed a dreadful night.

One of Seward's mental patients—a man named Renfield—was fatally attacked shortly after midnight. His dying words made Seward think the Count had broken into the building in search of Mina and that she was in great danger. Seward rushed to find Van Helsing, and together they broke into our room.

I was not aware of it.

Moonlight streamed through the window. They saw me lying on the bed in a stupor. Kneeling on the edge of it, facing outward, was Mina.

The Count was holding her wrists tight in one hand, and with the other hand pulling her face onto his chest. His skin was slashed across the ribs, and his blood trickled down. He was forcing my wife to drink it.

As Van Helsing and Seward burst in, the Count threw Mina back on the bed and sprang at them. But Van Helsing was holding a Holy Communion wafer in one hand and his crucifix in the other. The Count halted, and they advanced on him with both their crucifixes raised. As a cloud passed across the moon, the Count melted into mist and was gone.

Mina's wild scream was followed by a low, bleak wail and stirred me back to consciousness. She turned to me, but before I could embrace her, she drew back as if ashamed. Mina covered her face with her poor, crushed hands.

"Unclean!" she cried. "Unclean! I must touch and kiss you no more!"

"No, Mina," I said, pulling her toward me, wrapping her in my arms. "Nothing will ever come between us."

Van Helsing said gently, "Poor, dear Madam Mina. Tell us what happened so that we may live and learn."

She shivered, her face pressed to my chest. Then, taking a deep breath, she lifted her head and began:

"I took the sedative but for a long time could not sleep. Horrible thoughts crowded into my mind—of death and vampires and blood and pain.

But then I must have drifted off, for I didn't hear Jonathan coming in.

"When I woke, there was mist in the room, and Jonathan lay in the bed, but I could not wake him! As I watched, the mist became a man. He said I must keep silent—that if I made a noise, he would dash out Jonathan's brains.

"The man bared my throat. Held me so I could not move. He said he needed a little refreshment and pressed his reeking lips upon my neck. My strength was sucked from me. When he spoke again, his mouth dripped with my blood.

"He is so angry that we have dared to strike against him! And he is especially angry with me for helping you. With his nails, he tore open a vein in his chest and forced me to drink his blood. He has made me his creature now. I have no choice. Whenever he calls me, whatever he bids me do, I must obey."

The sun cannot have risen on any place more miserable in the entire world.

Late morning

Our sorrow over Mina cannot—must not—stop us doing what needs to be done. We must return to

Carfax to purify the boxes. We will then go on to the Count's London townhouse and do the same to the ones we find there. Van Helsing placed protections around Mina's room to keep her safe while we were away.

Just before we left, he said, "In the name of the Father, the Son, and the Holy Ghost," and pressed a piece of wafer to her forehead.

It seared her skin as if it were a branding iron.

Evening

There was no need to break into the Count's townhouse. Lord Arthur Godalming simply commanded a locksmith to open the front door while he stood on the doorstep and waited. It seems that no ordinary person dare question a lord. He can do exactly as he wishes.

Once inside, we found and purified all the boxes there.

One still remains undiscovered.

We were discussing where to search for it when the Count burst into the room. I threw myself in his path. The others advanced on him with the crucifix and wafer held aloft. His white, livid face turned a shade of greenish-yellow before he hurled himself at the window.

A crash. A glitter of falling glass and the Count was out.

He paused to call back at us, “You think you can defeat me? You puny creatures, with your faces like sheep? You will be sorry.”

The Count fixed his eyes on me then, and a devilish smile curled his lip. “The woman you love is mine. And others will join her. Soon I shall have an army of Undead to do my bidding.”

Then he was gone. I was devastated, but Van Helsing’s eyes gleamed with something that might have been hope.

“He fears us,” he said. “And now he has but one coffin-bed in which to hide.”

When we returned to Mina, we told her everything that had happened. We were fools to have excluded her for safety! In doing so, we had set her directly in the path of danger. I will never forgive myself for that.

When we had finished speaking, she said to us all very gently, “I know you must fight and destroy him, just as you did Lucy. The worst part of him must be killed so the best can have salvation. But do not do it in hate. Yes, he has brought all this misery, but that poor soul is the saddest of us all."

Mina glanced very briefly at Seward and then fixed her eyes on me. "Have pity in your heart when you finish him, as you would if you ever have to do the same for me."

I wept. How could I not? I was not alone. Our band of five brave, strong men all broke down in tears at Mina's feet.

October 3–4, midnight

Mina is sleeping, and sleeping without dreams. Her pity for Count Dracula has made my hatred seem despicable. She is so very good and kind and so much stronger than all of us. Surely God will preserve her? How could the world keep turning if Mina was not in it?

October 4, morning

Mina woke me. "Fetch Dr. Van Helsing," she whispered. "I have an idea."

I obeyed. As soon as he came in, she told him to hypnotize her: "Now, at once, before the sun rises. Now I can speak, and speak freely as myself! Be quick! The time is short!"

When she was in a trance, Van Helsing asked, "Where are you?"

In a dull, low monotone, she replied, "I don't know."

"What do you see?"

"Nothing. Dark."

"What do you hear?" Van Helsing pressed.

"Lapping water. Little waves slapping on wood. All around."

"Are you on a ship?"

"Yes," Mina said.

"What are you doing?"

"Nothing. I lie as still as death."

The sun rose over the horizon, and there was no more. Mina lay like a sleeping child for a few moments, then snapped awake.

"Did it work?" she asked.

"We have a clue," Van Helsing said with a grim smile. "The Count has escaped from this country. The hunt is on!"

"But if he has left England, can we not leave him be?" asked Mina. "Surely he will trouble us no more?"

Van Helsing's answer made my blood run cold.

“He can live for centuries, Madam Mina. Yet you are a mortal woman, for now at least. But since he put that mark upon your throat, your time as a human creature is running out.”

Mina’s Journal

October 5

The men have been to the port of London and made inquiries. They have deduced that the Count is in his last box and being carried along with the rest of the cargo in the hold of a ship called the *Czarina Catherine*. The vessel is bound for the port of Varna on the Black Sea. It was seen leaving on the ebbing tide, enveloped by a mist that seemed to move along with it.

Dracula has truly gone! A weight has been removed from me. I felt wonderfully at peace for a moment but then caught sight of myself in the mirror. I saw the red mark on my forehead and remembered Dr. Van Helsing’s words.

Later

I have seen the looks Dr. Seward and Dr. Van Helsing exchange. They do not trust me. It is painful, but they are probably right not to. I am the Count's creature, am I not? If I can see and hear what he does in my hypnotic state, might he use me in the same way?

The men met this evening to make plans, but I did not join them. I told Jonathan that I think it best if they talk without me.

Jonathan Harker's Journal

October 5, evening

It will take the *Czarina Catherine* three weeks or more to reach Varna. We can travel there over land in three days, armed against all natural and supernatural dangers, and confront the Count the moment the ship docks.

It was suggested at our meeting tonight that I should remain here with Mina. I have said I wish to talk to her before a decision is made.

She is sleeping calmly now, but I am so troubled I cannot rest.

Earlier, I told them that Mina thought it best if we talked without her, and no one questioned it. Yet she is the best and bravest of us all. How can we exclude her?

Later

Mina woke suddenly and demanded I make a promise that was as binding as our wedding vows.

"Promise me that you will not tell me anything from this time forward," she insisted. "Not a word or a look or a deed—not while this remains." She pointed to her scar.

I promised. I could do nothing else.

But I felt as if we were in different rooms and a huge oak door studded with nails had slammed shut between us.

October 6

Mina woke me early again and told me to fetch Van Helsing. When he arrived, she told him, "I must go with you on your journey."

Van Helsing was as surprised as I was. "Why?" he asked.

She pointed to her forehead. “This is why I must go. Dr. Van Helsing, you know that when the Count calls me, I must go to him. I will be in his control and capable of anything. I will cheat, steal, lie, kill. I will hurt anyone I am ordered to—even Jonathan will not be safe from me. But you will know when it comes—you will see the change in me. Before then, I can be of service. You can hypnotize me and discover what the Count sees and feels. It might tell you where he is going and what he plans to do. Let me be of some use.”

Van Helsing said very slowly and very gently, “Madam Mina, you shall come. We shall finish this together.”

Satisfied, Mina fell back on her pillow fast asleep.

Van Helsing and I went in search of the others. We made our travel plans and then parted company for the rest of the day. We needed to set our earthly affairs in order and write our wills before we left.

October 14

We are traveling to Varna. Mina is sleeping, with her head on my shoulder. The memory of what happened three days ago is going around and around my brain with the beat of the rocking train.

Three days ago, on the evening of October 11, Mina asked to see us all. She wanted us to swear an oath.

With such quiet dignity, she said, "You all must promise me—even you, my beloved husband—that if the time comes, you will kill me. If you are convinced that I have changed, and that it is better that my body dies so that I may live eternally, you must finish me. And when my body is dead, you must drive a stake through my heart and cut off my head and do whatever else is necessary."

There was a long, terrible silence. No one moved. But then Quincey Morris—that brave hero of the wild frontier—stepped forward. He kneeled down and swore he would do what Mina asked. She cried as she thanked him, and one by one, Van Helsing, Godalming, and Seward all kneeled and swore.

Still, I did not move. "Must I, too, make such a promise?" I asked Mina. My voice was nothing more than a whisper.

"You, too, my darling," she said, with great pity and tenderness. "You are nearest and dearest and all the world to me. Our souls are knit into one for all life and all time. If I must meet death this way, let it be done with kindness. Let it be your loving hand that finally sets me free."

So I made the promise, just like the others, and then Mina spoke again.

"Be warned. If the time comes, I will be your enemy. There can be no mercy, no delay. You must act fast."

And then she made another request.

She asked me to read the Burial Service over her.

"It would comfort me," Mina said.

How could I refuse?

How will I ever get the strange scene that followed out of my head? Its solemnity, its gloom, its sadness, horror, and terrible sweetness?

A funeral service held for a woman who still lived. A group of sorrowing friends kneeling around my sorrowing wife. My voice was so broken with emotion I had to keep stopping and gulping back tears.

It was so very painful. Yet we did it.

And Mina was right.

She is always right.

That strange ritual comforted us all, and the deep silence that followed afterward did not seem quite so full of despair.

PART 6
THE HUNT

Jonathan Harker's Journal

October 17, Varna

We traveled night and day and arrived here on October 15 about five o'clock. Mina sleeps a great deal, but at sunrise and sunset she is wakeful and alert. It has become the habit for Van Helsing to hypnotize Mina at these times. He always asks what she can see and hear, and the answers so far have remained the same—all is dark, and the water slaps against the ship's timbers.

Godalming has told the port authorities in Varna that he believes there is a coffin-size box in the *Czarina Catherine*'s cargo that contains something stolen from him. Once more, being a lord gives him an authority that no one dare question. Lord Godalming has permission to board the ship as soon as it docks to search the cargo. Officials will contact him the moment the ship is known to be approaching. If the *Czarina Catherine* arrives in daylight, we will be able to strike while the Count sleeps. If the ship docks at night, things will be much more difficult.

October 24

A whole week of waiting and not a word of news. At sunrise and sunset, Mina's hypnotic trances give the same answer: darkness, lapping waves, creaking timbers.

October 25

The *Czarina Catherine* has been sighted out at sea and will dock later this morning. We are in a fever of excitement but have said nothing to Mina. She has changed these past three weeks. The old Mina would have noticed our mood—there would have been no hiding our anticipation from those sharp, clever eyes of hers. This new Mina is dull and tired and has asked no questions.

Noon

No news yet of the ship's arrival. Mina has fallen into a heavy sleep.

Later

At sunset, Mina made the usual hypnotic report. The Count is still at sea.

October 26

Still no tidings of the *Czarina Catherine*. Mina's report is the same as always. It is possible that the ship is fogbound. Some of the vessels that came in on last night's tide reported seeing an odd, isolated patch of fog on their way to Varna.

October 27

Still no news. In her trances, Mina spoke of "rushing water" and added "small waves."

October 28

A telegram has arrived informing us that the *Czarina Catherine* has arrived in the port of

Galatz! It is more than two hundred miles away, and the only train that can take us there does not leave until 6:30 tomorrow morning. The Count has gotten away from us. Our plans must be revised.

Later

Darling Mina is more like her old self. It is a joy to see her suddenly awake and looking well.

"Something has shifted from me," Mina told us. "I feel freer than I have been of late!"

I was delighted until I saw Van Helsing glance at Seward. I had no idea what they were thinking, but Mina seemed to understand that look and spoke again.

"The Count knows we are in pursuit of him," she said. "He felt me inside his mind, I think, and has now freed me so I can't inform on him."

I thought Van Helsing would be downcast or frustrated by this development, but he was not. In fact, his eyes sparkled with excitement, for he believes that the bond forced on Mina by the Count when he made her his creature means that he cannot cut himself off from her entirely. Van Helsing is certain that when hypnotized, Mina will still be able to see with the Count's eyes and hear with his ears. My wife is a weapon that might yet prove lethal to Dracula. But at what cost to herself? At what cost? Dear God, at what cost?

October 29

We are on the train bound for Galatz. It was due to arrive at two in the morning but is already running three hours late. We are in an agony of suspense.

It took longer than usual for Mina to sink into a trance this morning. When she did, the information was confusing. "We are still. No waves. Water running. Creaking wood. Clunking . . ."

And this evening she said, "Cold wind. Men talking. Falling water. Wolves howl."

October 30

At sunrise this morning, Mina said, "Water swirling, creaking, clunking, wood on wood. Cattle lowing."

Later

We have arrived in Galatz.

Quincey Morris has taken Mina to the hotel and will stay with her. He speaks no foreign languages so can be of no help with our investigations.

Godalming has gone to the British Embassy. Van Helsing, Seward, and I have talked to the captain of the *Czarina Catherine* and to various others.

Now, at the end of the day, the only thing we have discovered is that the box was taken off the ship long before we reached Galatz and moved on elsewhere. We cannot discover whether the box was loaded onto another vessel or a different mode of transport. We have no idea in which direction Dracula is bound.

Mina's Journal

October 30

I have been thinking about the things I said in my hypnotic trances. I'm told that I talked of cattle lowing, water swirling, creaking wood. It sounds as if the Count is still in his coffin-box and is still on a boat. But if there is no sound of lapping waves, perhaps he isn't at sea anymore. Could he be on a different body of water? A lake perhaps. Or a river?

A river seems most likely. A boat propelled by oars or poles would creak and clunk if being worked against the current. There would be no such sounds if it were simply floating downstream. In which case, surely he is being taken inland?

I have consulted a map.

There are two rivers that seem to be possible. One is very easily navigated. The second is much more difficult, but it does run up around the Borgo Pass. It winds and loops and turns back on itself, then runs as close to Dracula's castle as can be reached by water.

When the men returned, I explained my reasoning to them. Jonathan took me in his arms and kissed me.

Dr. Van Helsing said, "Our dear Madam Mina is a teacher to us all. Her eyes have seen where we were blind. We will go after the Count. If we can reach him by day while he is on the water, our task will be over."

Plans have been made. Lord Godalming is to hire a steamboat and take it upriver. Mr. Morris and Dr. Seward will obtain horses and ride along the bank in case the Count comes onto land.

Jonathan wished to stay with me, but it is best he go with Lord Godalming as Jonathan is young and strong. I am to travel with Dr. Van Helsing along the very same route that Jonathan traveled when he first went to Castle Dracula.

I am well aware that Jonathan is very afraid for me. I am going into the jaws of death, but there is nothing else I can do. If the Count eludes us again, we all know what will happen to me. It will happen to us all.

We must not fail.

Later

It is very lucky for us that Lord Godalming is a rich man and is happy to spend his money freely. Wealth and a noble title can achieve such wonders! We are all fully equipped for our journeys, and now our band of six must divide.

Dr. Van Helsing and I are to take the train to Veresti and buy horses and a carriage there. We will drive ourselves, for we dare trust no one as we draw closer to Castle Dracula.

It has taken all my courage to say goodbye to my darling husband. I am so afraid that Jonathan and I may never meet again.

I keep telling myself, *Be brave, Mina!* There must be no more tears now unless God smiles on us and my tears are happy and triumphant ones.

November 1

When we started our journey, I thought this a beautiful country. I kept imagining Jonathan and I traveling through it alone together under happy circumstances and how delightful it would all be! The people here are kind and strong. It would be so interesting for us to spend time with them, learning their ways and customs.

But then we stopped to change horses, and when I briefly removed my hat and veil, a woman saw the scar on my forehead and screamed. She crossed herself and held out two fingers toward me to ward off the evil eye.

Since then, I have kept my hat firmly on my head and my veil tightly over my face. But there are so few strangers like us here that I imagine rumor will run ahead of us and we will be treated everywhere with fear and suspicion.

November 2, morning

We traveled at good speed all day yesterday and took turns driving all night. Today is bright but cold, and I feel a strange heaviness in the air. Yesterday, I said the same when I was hypnotized: "Darkness, swirling water, creaking wood."

But this morning, Dr. Van Helsing told me I said, "Darkness, creaking wood, roaring water." The river is changing.

I pray and pray and pray that Jonathan is safe.

Night

The country gets wilder and more savage looking. By morning, we should reach the Borgo Pass. What will tomorrow bring?

November 3

When we reached the Borgo Pass, Dr. Van Helsing seemed not to know which direction he should steer the horses. So I pointed and said, "That way."

"You know that?" he asked, looking surprised and a little concerned.

“Of course I do!” I said. “Jonathan traveled this road. He wrote about it in his journal, didn’t he? You and I have both read it.”

Dr. Van Helsing gave his head a small shake as if he thought my reply strange, but I didn’t see why. There was only one road it could be!

We went on and on, slow and steady until sunset. Dr. Van Helsing tried to hypnotize me as usual with no effect. Then the sun sank very suddenly behind a mountain. We were plunged into darkness. Dr. Van Helsing took a sharp indrawn breath as if he was startled by it. For some reason, I found it funny, and so I laughed, which unsettled him even more.

Dr. Van Helsing then started a fire, unharnessed the horses, fed and then tethered them so they might graze. While he was busy, I prepared our supper but found I had no appetite. Dr. Van Helsing was looking at me so strangely when I handed him his food that I lied and said I’d eaten while he was tending to the horses. I don’t think he believed me. All night he was twitchy and alert and kept glancing in my direction, so I didn’t sleep until sunrise.

November 4

It is getting colder, and the gray sky is heavy with snow. The horses kept trudging on their way, and both of us must have fallen asleep. Dr. Van Helsing woke with such a start that I was jerked awake, too. We looked about us and found we were starting to climb a very steep slope.

Ahead—perhaps half a mile or so away—we could see Castle Dracula standing on the summit, outlined against the setting sun.

We stopped for the night.

Once more, Dr. Van Helsing made a fire and tended to the horses while I prepared food. Again, I had no appetite. And this time I did not trouble myself to lie to him. In truth, I was beginning to feel rather strange.

Dr. Van Helsing was looking at me as if I was something to fear.

He broke a Holy Communion wafer in his hands, and the very sight of it made me feel ill. I watched him crumble it very fine and then scatter it in a large circle around me. I made no move to stop him because I could not. I seemed rooted to the spot and felt very odd indeed. Dizzy. Sick.

It was only a circle of crumbs, but I felt as if a great iron wall enclosed me and I was weighed down with iron chains and there was no way out. Yet Dr. Van Helsing could step freely back and forth across it. When it was complete, he came inside the circle and joined me.

The night passed very slowly.

In the coldest hour, the fire began to die. Flurries of snow came whirling and flying. With them was a chill mist that slowly, slowly, slowly took the shapes of women. These were women I recognized. The women from Castle Dracula. My sisters. My future.

The terrified horses screamed and tore at their tethers.

Dr. Van Helsing would have gone to free them, but I caught his hand and held him back.

"Stay here where you are safe!" I said.

"It's you I fear for," he cried.

I laughed in his face. "Why fear for me?" I said. "There is no one in the world safer from them than I am."

The women started calling to me, "Come, sister. Come to us. Come!"

But I could not step outside that circle any more than they could come in. They called and called, but as they called, Jonathan's face came into my mind. It was so clear—as if he stood between myself and them. And I recalled how he had longed for them to kiss him and what the women would have done to him. A rage came into my heart so strong that all other thoughts and feelings were banished.

Dr. Van Helsing was staring at me, his face full of terror. But something in my eyes must have told him of the hatred, the fury, the revulsion I felt for those three sisters of mine. I was not one of them. Not now. I would never be while my heart and soul were Jonathan's.

Dr. Van Helsing and I remained within that holy circle until the red light of dawn began to streak the sky and my sisters melted away in the mist and snow.

We lived. But the poor horses had all died from sheer terror.

November 5

At sunrise, I slept. While I was safe within the holy circle, Dr. Van Helsing walked to the castle. He found his way to the old chapel that Jonathan had described in his journal. He searched every tomb until he found the coffins where the three women lay sleeping. Dr. Van Helsing did what was necessary. It was butcher work. But he came back certain that Dracula was the only vampire left in existence.

Dr. Van Helsing returned to the circle and sat in silence while I slept on.

I woke very suddenly around half an hour before sunset.

"Jonathan is almost here!" I cried. "They are all coming to meet us!"

November 6

From our vantage point, Dr. Van Helsing and I could see across a vast distance. Down below us, the river was glinting as it wound around the trees. From its valley came a group of men. They all wore the same wide hats, nail-studded belts, sheepskin coats, and high boots just as Jonathan had described in his journal. They drove a wagon on which lay a coffin-box and were whipping the horses, galloping them as hard as they could toward the castle.

Daylight was fading fast.

I knew very well that at the moment of sunset, the creature in that box would escape. Here, in his homeland, he would elude all mortal pursuit!

All was lost! I felt a moment of wild despair.

Then I saw that two horsemen were following the wagon, drawing ever closer to it—Mr. Morris and Dr. Seward. But where was Jonathan? There. There! And Lord Godalming was coming up on the other side of the slope, riding at breakneck speed.

They were all approaching the wagon. And it was coming closer and closer to Dr. Van Helsing and I. He loaded his rifle. I loaded my revolver.

Suddenly, there was the terrible howling of wolves. Close. Getting closer. Wind blew in fierce gusts, driving the snow with its fury. Nearer and nearer the men drew, but the sun sank lower and lower.

"Halt!" cried Jonathan. The men driving the wagon reined their horses in. Lord Godalming and Jonathan dashed upon it from one side, Dr. Seward and Mr. Morris from the other.

There came flashing knives, howling wolves, gunshots—all was chaos.

Jonathan jumped upon the wagon. With almost inhuman strength, he raised the great box and flung it off, onto the ground.

Where there was blood. So much of it! Red. In the snow. Whose blood? Who was hurt? I could not see. Jonathan? I could not help but run toward him.

Jonathan had not seen me. Together, he and Quincey Morris were prying the lid from the box.

The Count lay there. Perfectly still. Sleeping.

I breathed a sigh of relief.

But then the Count's eyes snapped open and reflected in them was the setting sun. Those eyes shone with triumph as he looked toward me and began to rise from his coffin.

The Count called me. And the call was irresistible.

Time itself slowed down.

I saw—and I felt—Jonathan plunging his knife into the Count's neck. I saw—and I felt—Quincey Morris thrust his dagger into the Count's heart.

I saw—and I felt—the Count take a single breath. His eyes drilled into mine for a split second that seemed to last an eternity. Then Dracula's whole body crumbled into dust.

But in that last look, just before his destruction, there was a look of sublime relief on his face. Of absolute peace.

I suppose the men who had driven the wagon fled along with the wolves.

All I remember now is that our band of six were alone on that mountain.

And one of us was dying.

Not Jonathan.

Quincey Morris. His life was flowing away through a great gaping wound in his side.

I sank to my knees beside him in the snow and took his hand in mine. When I began to weep, Quincey said gently, "Don't cry for me, ma'am."

The setting sun was bathing everything in red light, including my face, I suppose. For Quincey suddenly pointed to my forehead.

"My life has not been given in vain! See the mark?" Quincey called. "It's gone! Mina is saved. The curse is lifted. God be thanked."

We five were left to grieve as Quincey Morris died with a smile and in silence. He died the noble hero of his own thrilling story and a very gallant gentleman.

NOTE

Seven years ago, we all went through the flames of hell. The happiness of the survivors since then is well worth the pain we suffered. It is an added joy to Mina and me that our boy was born on the anniversary of Morris's death. I know his mother holds the secret belief that some of our brave friend's spirit has passed into our son. He has been named after each and every one of our little band of men, but we just call him Quincey.

In the summer of this year, we made a journey to Transylvania and visited places full of vivid and terrible memories. It was almost impossible to believe that the things we had seen and heard had truly happened. Every trace of them had been blotted out.

When we got home, we met with Godalming and Seward, both now happily married, and with Van Helsing. We talked of the old times, and then I said,

"We can never tell our story to anyone! Who would believe such a wild, fantastical tale?"

Van Helsing was sitting with our child on his knee and summed up everyone's feelings. "We ask no one to believe us but this boy. He will someday know what a brave and gallant woman his mother is. He already knows her sweetness and loving care. Later, he will understand how some men loved her so much that they risked their lives for her sake."

JONATHAN HARKER

Our books are tested
for children and young people by
children and young people.

Thanks to everyone who consulted on
a manuscript for their time and effort in
helping us to make our books better
for our readers.

Read all these exciting classic tales from Everyone Can Be a Reader!

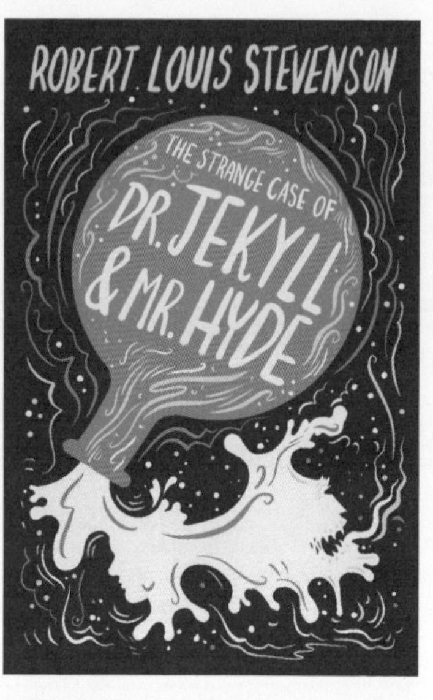

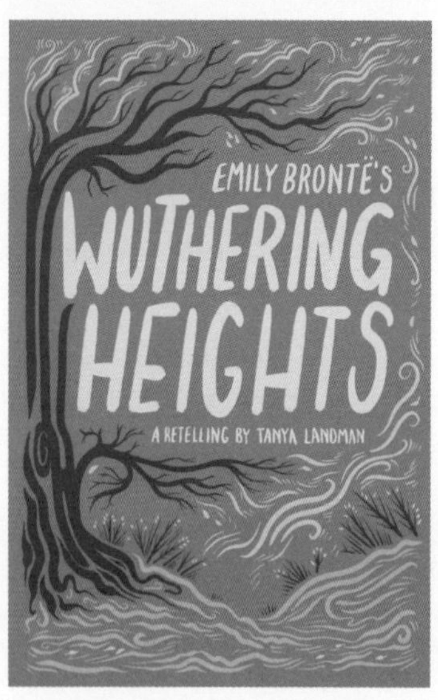

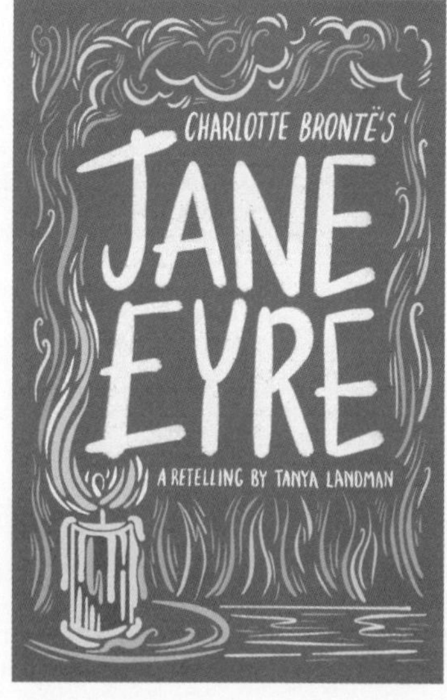

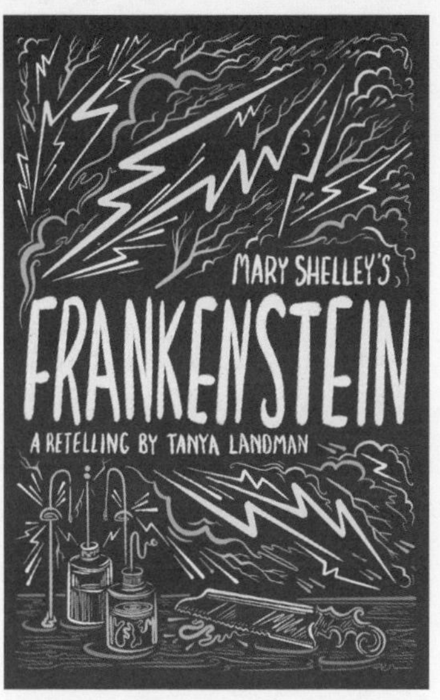
MARY SHELLEY'S
FRANKENSTEIN
A RETELLING BY TANYA LANDMAN

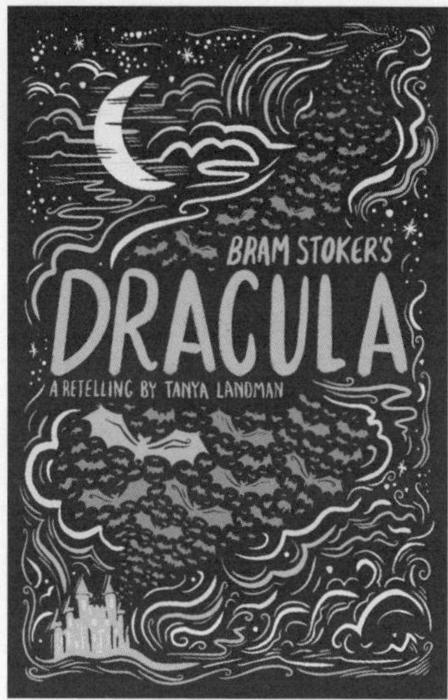
BRAM STOKER'S
DRACULA
A RETELLING BY TANYA LANDMAN

LOUISA MAY ALCOTT'S
LITTLE WOMEN
A RETELLING BY LAURA WOOD

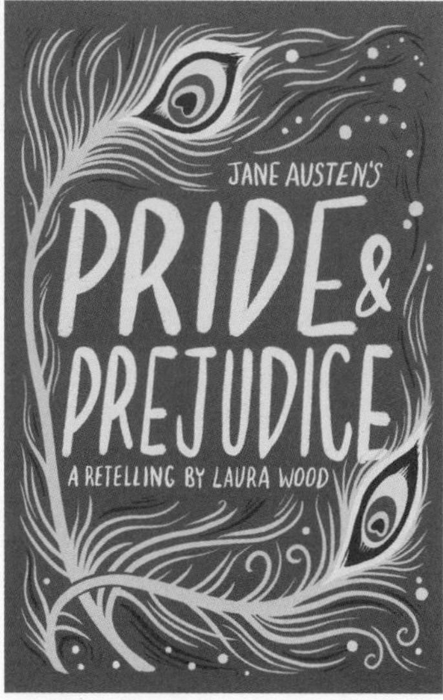
JANE AUSTEN'S
PRIDE & PREJUDICE
A RETELLING BY LAURA WOOD